ABOUT THE BANK STREET READY-TO-READ SERIES

Seventy years of educational research and innovative teaching have given the Bank Street College of Education the reputation as America's most trusted name in early childhood education.

Because no two children are exactly alike in their development, we have designed the *Bank Street Ready-to-Read* series in three levels to accommodate the individual stages of reading readiness of children ages four through eight.

- *Level 1:* GETTING READY TO READ—read-alouds for children who are taking their first steps toward reading.
- *Level 2:* READING TOGETHER—for children who are just beginning to read by themselves but may need a little help.
- *Level 3:* I CAN READ IT MYSELF—for children who can read independently.

Our three levels make it easy to select the books most appropriate for a child's development and enable him or her to grow with the series step by step. The *Bank Street Ready-to-Read* books also overlap and reinforce each other, further encouraging the reading process.

We feel that making reading fun and enjoyable is the single most important thing that you can do to help children become good readers. And we hope you'll be a part of Bank Street's long tradition of learning through sharing.

The Bank Street College of Education

W9-APV-314

"NOT NOW!" SAID THE COW
A Bantam Little Rooster Book
Simultaneous paper-over-board and trade paper editions/July 1989

Little Rooster is a trademark of Bantam Books,
a division of Bantam Doubleday Dell Publishing Group, Inc.

Series graphic design by Alex Jay/Studio J
Associate Editor: Randall Reich

Special thanks to James A. Levine, Betsy Gould,
Erin B. Gathrid, and Whit Stillman.

Library of Congress Cataloging-in-Publication Data
Oppenheim, Joanne.
"Not now!" said the cow.

(Bank Street ready-to-read)
"A Byron Preiss Book."
"A Bantam little rooster book."
Summary: In this story based on "The Little Red Hen,"
a little black crow asks his animal friends to help
with the planting of some corn seed.
[1. Folklore]   I. Demarest, Chris L., ill
II. Title.   III. Series.
PZ8.1.057No   1989   398.2'4528817 [E]   88-7957
ISBN 0-553-05826-6
ISBN 0-553-34691-1 (pbk.)

Bantam Books are published by Bantam Books, a division of Bantam Dou-
bleday Dell Publishing Group, Inc. Its trademark, consisting of the words
"Bantam Books" and the portrayal of a rooster, is Registered in U.S. Patent
and Trademark Office and in other countries. Marca Registrada. Bantam
Books, 666 Fifth Avenue, New York, New York 10103.

PRINTED IN THE UNITED STATES OF AMERICA

WAK 0 9 8

Bank Street Ready-to-Re

"Not Now!" Said the Cow

by Joanne Oppenheim
Illustrated by Chris Demarest

A Byron Preiss Book

A BANTAM LITTLE ROOSTER BOOK
NEW YORK · TORONTO · LONDON · SYDNEY · AUCKLAND

One day a little black crow
spotted a sack of corn seed
lying on the ground.

ALL BY MYSELF.''

"No, no!" cawed Crow.
"I planted the seeds.
I pulled the weeds.
When the corn was tall,
I picked it all.
I shucked it, shelled it,
and built the fire.
I shook the pot
til it got hot.
And now I'll eat
this nice, hot popcorn. . .

"Where's my share?" whinnied Mare.
"I'll take that!" meowed the Cat.
"That's my job," grunted Hog.
"Yummy, yummy,"
squealed the Bunny.
"For me! For me!" brayed Donkey.
"First licks," peeped the Chicks.
"Let's eat," baaed the Sheep.
"Oh, wow!" mooed Cow.

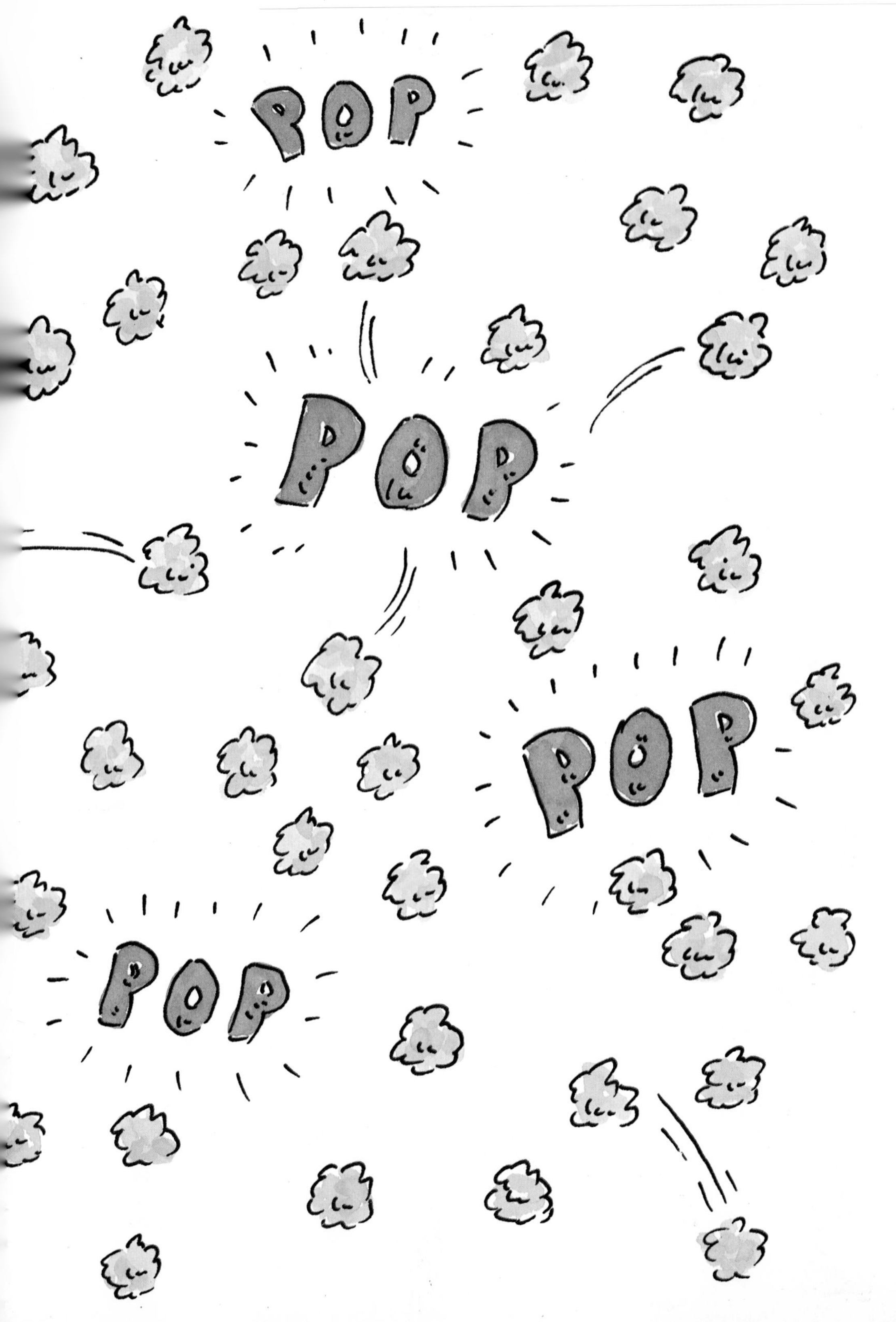
POP
POP
POP
POP

So the little black crow
shook the corn in the pot. . . .
He shook it and shook it
til the pot got hot. . . .

And suddenly,
inside that pot,
the corn got hot
and would not stop.
It just kept going. . .

"I can't do that," meowed the Cat.
"Not my job," grunted Hog.
"Don't be funny," squealed the Bunny.
"Why me?" brayed Donkey.
"Nix, nix!" peeped the Chicks.
"I'm asleep," baaed the Sheep.
"Not now," mooed Cow.

"Oh," cawed Crow. "Then I will do it
ALL BY MYSELF."

Soon the wood was burning hot, and
the little black crow put a top on the pot.

"Who will help me shake the pot?"

"I don't dare!" whinnied Mare.

"Not my job," grunted Hog.
"Don't be funny," squealed the Bunny.
"Why me?" brayed Donkey.
"Nix, nix!" peeped the Chicks.
"I'm asleep," baaed the Sheep.
"Not now," mooed Cow.

"Oh," cawed Crow. "Then I will do it
ALL BY MYSELF."

Then Crow put the corn into a pot.
"What we need," he said,
"is a fire that's hot.

Who will help me gather wood?"

"I can't do that," meowed the Cat.

"Nix, nix!"
peeped the Chicks.

"I'm asleep,"
baaed the Sheep.

"Not now," mooed Cow.

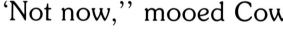

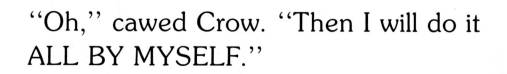

"Oh," cawed Crow. "Then I will do it
ALL BY MYSELF."

"Not my job,"
grunted Hog.

"Don't be funny,"
squealed the Bunny.

"Why me?"
brayed Donkey.

Now all that corn was still on the cob,
and taking it off was a big, big job.

"Who will help me shell the corn?"

"I'm asleep,"
baaed the Sheep.

"Not now," mooed Cow.

"Oh," cawed Crow. "Then I will do it
ALL BY MYSELF."

"Caw, caw!" he crowed.
"Just what we need—
a sack of seed!"

So the little black crow
flew back to the farm.

"Caw, caw!" he crowed.
"Look what I found just lying around.
Who will help me plant
these seeds in the ground?"

"Not now," mooed Cow.

"I'm asleep," baaed the Sheep.

"Oh," cawed Crow. "Then I will do it ALL BY MYSELF."

Soon the sprouts were tall and green,
but weeds were growing in between.

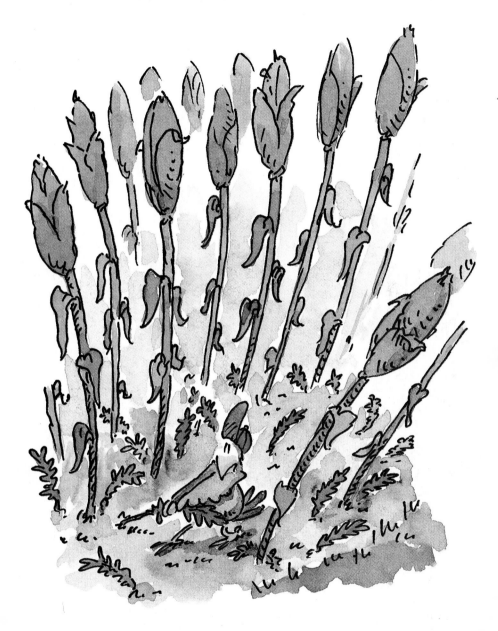

"Who will help me pull the weeds?"

"Nix, nix!" peeped the Chicks.

"I'm asleep,"
baaed the Sheep.

"Not now," mooed Cow.

"Oh," cawed Crow. "Then I will do it
ALL BY MYSELF."

The rows of corn grew tall and thick.
Soon, fat green ears were ready to pick.

"Who will help me pick the corn?"

"Why me?" brayed Donkey.

"Nix, nix!" peeped the Chicks.

"I'm asleep,"
baaed the Sheep.

"Not now,"
mooed Cow.

"Oh," cawed Crow. "Then I will do it
ALL BY MYSELF."

Crow picked the ears one by one,
and late that night his work was done.

"Who will help me shuck the corn?"

"Don't be funny,"
squealed the Bunny.

"Why me?"
brayed Donkey.

"Nix, nix!" peeped the Chicks.